The Ladybird Key Words Reading Scheme is based on these commonly used words. Those used most often in the English language are introduced first—with other words of popular appeal to children. All the Key Words list is covered in the early books, and the later titles use further word lists to develop full reading fluency. The total number of different words which will be learned in the complete reading scheme is nearly two thousand. The gradual introduction of these words, frequent repetition and complete 'carry-over' from book to book, will ensure rapid learning.

The full colour illustrations have been designed to create a desirable attitude towards learning— by making every child *eager* to read each title. Thus this attractive reading scheme embraces not only the latest findings in word frequency, but also the natural interests and activities of happy children.

Each book contains a list of the new words introduced.

W MURRAY, the author of the Ladybird Key Words Reading Scheme, is an experienced headmaster, author and lecturer on the teaching of reading. He is co-author, with J McNally, of Key Words to Literacy — *a teacher's book published by The Teacher Publishing Co Ltd.*

LADYBIRD KEY WORDS READING SCHEME has 12 graded books in each of its three series—'a', 'b' and 'c'. As explained in the handbook *Teaching Reading*, these 36 graded books are all written on a controlled vocabulary, and take the learner from the earliest stages of reading to reading fluency.

The 'a' series gradually introduces and repeats new words. The parallel 'b' series gives the needed further repetition of these words at each stage, but in a different context and with different illustrations.

The 'c' series is also parallel to the 'a' series, and supplies the necessary link with writing and phonic training.

An illustrated booklet—*Notes for using the Ladybird Key Words Reading Scheme*—can be obtained free from the publishers. This booklet fully explains the Key Words principle. It also includes information on the reading books, work books and apparatus available, and such details as the vocabulary loading and reading ages of all books.

BOOK 4c
The Ladybird Key Words Reading Scheme

Say the sound

by W MURRAY
with illustrations by J H WINGFIELD

Ladybird Books Loughborough

We can read the words—

boy

ball

boat

bus

Look at each picture and make the sound of the letter.

b

b

b

b

We can read the words—

car

cow

cat

cake

Look at each picture and make the sound of the letter.

C

C

C

C

Complete the words as you write them
in your exercise book.
The pictures will help you.

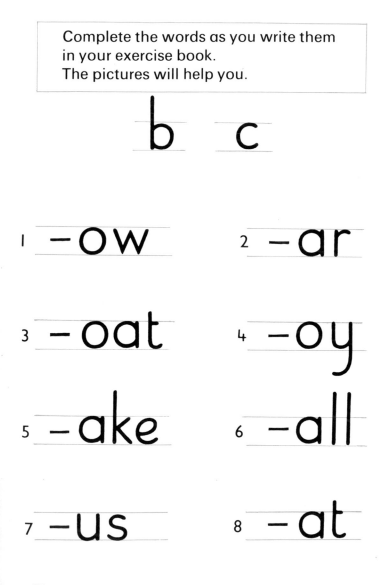

b   c

1 – o w

2 – a r

3 – o a t

4 – o y

5 – a k e

6 – a l l

7 – u s

8 – a t

The answers are on Page 50

1

2

3

4

5

6

7

8

We can read the words—

tea

two

top

toys

Look at each picture and make the sound of the letter.

t

t 2

t

t

a

1. An apple.

2. The girl has an apple.

3. The girl draws an apple.
   She writes **a** for apple.
   She makes the sound for **a**.

4. The boy draws an apple.
   He draws **a** for apple.
   He makes the sound for **a**.

Complete the words as you write them in your exercise book.
The pictures will help you.

b c t a

1 —pple

2 —wo

3 —an

4 —ea

5 —pples

6 —op

7 —oys

8 —ed

The answers are on Page 50

1

2

3

4

5

6

7

8

The girl is at school.

She likes school.

She has some pictures.

She puts the pictures with
the sounds.

"I like to do this," the girl says.
"It helps me to read."

"This helps me to read," says the boy.

He is at school.

He likes school.

The boy has some pictures.

He puts the pictures with the sounds.

Here is a girl at work.

She makes a picture with
the cards.

She makes the sounds for **c**, **a**, **t**.

"**C**, **a**, **t** makes cat," she says.

She draws a cat, and then
she writes.

Here is a boy at work.

He makes a picture with
the cards.

He makes the sounds for **b**, **a**, **t**.

"**B**, **a**, **t** makes bat," he says.

He draws a bat, and then
he writes.

The boy and the girl play a game with the cards.

They play a game with pictures and sounds.

The girl can see the pictures.

The boy can see the letters.

"Point to bat," says the girl.

"Is this it?" says the boy.

"Have a look," she says.

The boy looks at his card.

"Yes," he says, "it has a picture of a bat."

He keeps the card.

"Point to a cat," says the girl.

He points to a card with **c**.

"This is it," he says.

"Yes," says the girl, "that is the one."

We can read the words—

four

five

fire

fish

Look at each picture and make the sound of the letter.

f 4

f 5

f

f

We can read the words—

hat

hand

horse

house

Look at each picture and make the sound of the letter.

h

h

h

h

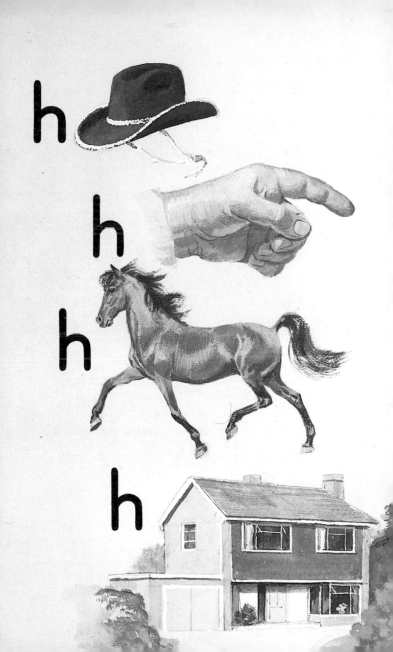

Complete the words as you write them in your exercise book.
The pictures will help you.

f h

1 – ouse

2 – our

3 – ive

4 – at

5 – and

6 – ish

7 – ire

8 – orse

The answers are on Page 50

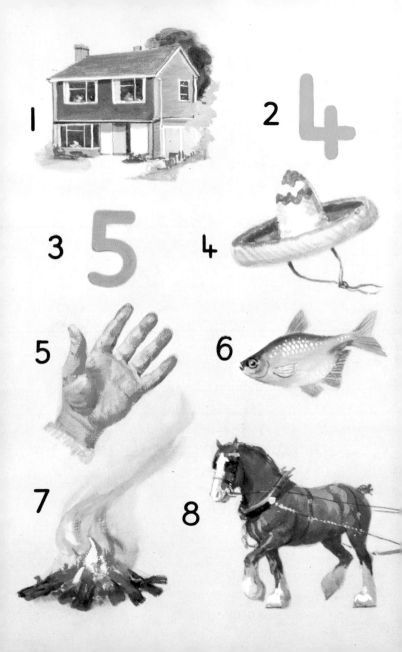

We can read the words—

man

milk

money

men

Look at each picture and make the sound of the letter.

m

m

m

m

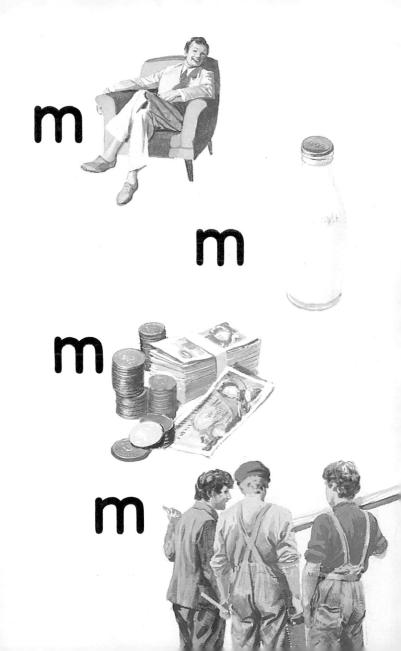

We can read the words—

sea

saw

seat

sun

Look at each picture and make the sound of the letter.

Complete the words as you write them
in your exercise book.
The pictures will help you.

m   s

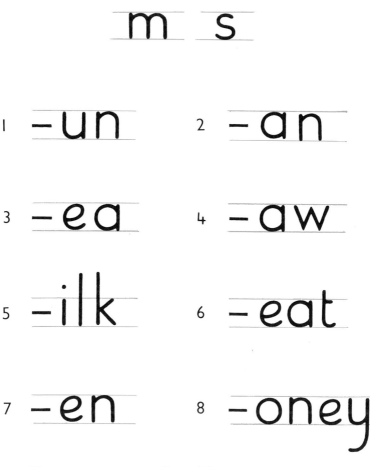

1 -un   2 -an

3 -ea   4 -aw

5 -ilk   6 -eat

7 -en   8 -oney

The answers are on Page 50

The girl has some letters.

She makes the sounds of the letters and reads the words.

She reads the word **at**.

Then she makes the sound of the letter **b** and makes **b—at**.

"**B—at** makes bat," she says, "and I see that **c—at** makes cat, **b—all** makes ball, **c—an** makes can, and **b—us** makes bus."

at at

cat bat

an all

can ball

us

bus

The boy has some letters.

He makes the sounds of the letters and reads the words.

He reads the word **at**.

Then he makes the sound of the letter **h** and makes **h—at**.

"**H—at** makes hat," he says, "and I see that **f—at** makes fat, **h—is** makes his, **r—an** makes ran, and **m—an** makes man."

The children all help to make a big fire at the farm. The man lets the boys and girls have some things for the fire.

"We do not want to get into danger," says Jane to the little girl. "We'll keep away."

"There will be no danger," says Peter.

Copy out and complete—

1. The children are — t the farm.

2. They — ake a big fire.

3. The man — elps the children.

4. He gives the children
   — ome things
   for the fire.

The answers are on Page 51

Here is the fire. "It's for us," says Peter. All the children like the big fire.

Jane keeps the little girl with her. They are not in danger.

The dog Pat is here. He is with Jane. He will not jump up or go away.

Copy out and complete—

1. Peter — nd Jane are here.

2. They — an see the fire.

3. They like the — ig fire.

4. They have — un.

The answers are on Page 51

A car stops. The children see it.

"I can see my Dad," says Jane. "He has come to take us home."

They thank Pam and then they all go off home with Dad in his car.

"What fun it was," says Jane to him.